All Are Equal:

The Essential Gender Equality Guide

Priyanka Verma

AF529982

DIAMOND BOOKS

www.diamondbooks.in

© Publisher

Publisher : **Diamond Pocket Books (P) Ltd.**
X-30, Okhla Industrial Area, Phase-II
New Delhi-110020
Phone : 011-40712200
E-mail : wecare@diamondbooks.in
Website : www.diamondbooks.in
Edition : 2025
Printed By : Repro (India)

Preface

In today's world, where diversity is our strength, it is essential that children grow up understanding the value of equality, fairness, and respect for all genders. This book is a joyful, engaging journey that introduces gender equality in a way that is age-appropriate, relatable, and deeply meaningful.

Aligned with the principles of the National Education Policy 2020, this guide encourages critical thinking, social awareness, and empathy through stories, activities, and real-life examples. Our aim is to build a generation of thoughtful, respectful, and inclusive individuals who understand that equality starts with small everyday actions.

Priyanka Verma

Foreword

By an educator, psychologist, or gender rights advocate

Every child deserves to grow up knowing they are valued—not just for what they do, but for who they are. Gender equality is not just a social issue—it's a life skill. It helps children learn cooperation, empathy, and leadership. This book bridges the gap between understanding and action by making the concept of gender equality relatable, interactive, and inspiring. A must-read for students, educators, and families alike.

Contents

Chapter 1

Let's Talk – What is Gender?

Let's Begin

A Curious Day at the Toy Store
Anaya and her younger brother Aarav walk into a bright, colorful toy shop. Aarav rushes to the shelf with toy trucks. Anaya picks up a shiny blue robot. Just then, another child in the shop says, "Robots are for boys. Don't you like dolls?"

Anaya frowns. "But I like robots too." Aarav hears this and replies, "I wish I could try the pink cooking set, but everyone says it's only for girls."

Have you ever wanted to do something, wear something, or play something—but stopped because someone said it's not meant for your gender?
This chapter is where we begin to question such beliefs.

Explore

What is Gender?
Gender is how society thinks boys and girls—or men and women—should behave, dress, talk, and live. These ideas often come from culture, traditions, and media, not from facts.

Gender is not the same as biological sex, which is assigned at birth (male or female) based on physical differences.

Let's look at the difference:

Biological Sex	Gender
Based on physical traits like body parts	Based on roles and expectations
Assigned at birth	Learned from society
Male / Female	Boyish, girlish, or beyond
Cannot be changed easily	Can change over time and choice

People can express their gender in many ways. Some boys may like cooking. Some girls may love karate. And that's perfectly okay.

Common Gender Ideas (and why we should rethink them)

Have you heard these before?
- "Girls should be soft and polite."
- "Boys should not cry."
- "Blue is for boys, pink is for girls."
- "Girls are not good at science."
- "Boys should not play with dolls."

These are called gender stereotypes—ideas that limit people based on gender. And they are often wrong, unfair, and harmful.

Let's bust some myths:

Stereotype	Truth
Boys are stronger	Everyone is strong in their own way
Girls talk more	Talking is not based on gender
Boys don't cry	Everyone has emotions
Girls can't lead	Leadership is for everyone
Only boys play sports	Girls are amazing athletes too

When we believe in these stereotypes, we stop ourselves and others from being free, happy, and confident.

Why Gender Matters in Childhood

Children begin noticing gender roles as early as 3 years old. By age 7, many children already believe that some jobs, toys, or clothes are only for a certain gender.

This affects how children:
- See themselves ("I'm not good at math because I'm a girl.")
- Treat others ("Boys don't play kitchen games!")
- Choose dreams ("I can't be a scientist. That's a boy's job.")

When we teach children that anyone can do anything, we help them build confidence, fairness, and kindness.

Try It

Activity 1: "True or Just a Stereotype?"

Below are some sentences.

Read them and decide whether they are based on facts or stereotypes:

1. Girls can be doctors.

2. Boys should not wear earrings.
3. Only girls like to dance.
4. Boys can be chefs.
5. Girls can't climb trees.
6. Everyone should be kind.

Now go through your answers. Discuss with a friend or teacher.

Which ideas are truly fair?

Activity 2: "Draw Yourself Free"
Make a drawing of yourself doing something you love—even if others say it's not meant for your gender.

For example:
- A girl fixing a car
- A boy caring for a baby
- A child painting with all the colors they love

Display it proudly with the title: "This Is Me!"

Activity 3: "Who Does What?"

Make a list of chores and jobs at home or school. Like:
- Cooking
- Sweeping
- Helping a younger sibling
- Using a computer
- Playing sports

Who usually does these in your house? Now ask:
"Can anyone do these jobs?"
If the answer is YES, you're thinking like a gender equality champion.

Think & Reflect

Let's pause and ask some big questions:

1. Have you ever stopped yourself from doing something you loved because of what others might say?
2. How do you feel when someone tells you what you should do because you're a boy or a girl?
3. What can you say to a friend who says, "That's only for boys/girls"?

Reflection helps us understand that everyone deserves the freedom to explore and express themselves.

Let's Revise

Let's wrap up what we've learned so far:

- Gender is about how people behave or are expected to behave in society.
- It is not the same as biological sex.
- Stereotypes are unfair ideas that limit people.
- Everyone should be free to express themselves and follow their interests, no matter their gender.
- Children should be encouraged to be who they are without fear or shame.

Check Yourself

Multiple Choice Questions:

1. What is gender?

(a) A color
(b) A way society expects people to behave based on whether they are boys or girls ✔
(c) A toy
(d) None of the above

2. Which of these is a stereotype?

(a) Boys are always stronger than girls ✔
(b) Everyone needs food
(c) Some people are tall
(d) Math is a school subject

3. Choose the fair statement:

(a) Girls should always wear dresses
(b) Boys can never cry
(c) Children can choose what they like, no matter their gender ✔
(d) Pink is only for girls

Short Answer:

1. Name one stereotype you've heard.
2. Why do you think it is unfair?
3. What would you say to someone who tells you "Boys don't do that"?

Beyond the Book

Let's take this learning into the real world!
Project: "Voices from My Home"

Step 1: Ask three family members or neighbors:
"Do you think boys and girls should have the same rights and choices?"

Step 2: Write down their answers.

Step 3: In your class or with friends, talk about:

- Were the answers similar or different?
- Why do some people still believe in stereotypes?
- What can we do to spread the message of equality?

Digital Extension (QR Code Placeholder)

Watch: "Children Speak on Gender Roles" – A short video of kids around the world sharing their thoughts on what boys and girls can do.

Final Thought

You are not just a boy or girl—you are a person with dreams, choices, and strength. What matters most is how you think, how you treat others, and how you feel about yourself.
Let's promise to support every child, every friend, and every family member to be who they are—without limits.

Chapter 2

What is Gender Equality?

Let's Begin

A Day in the Life: Two Friends, Two Worlds

Ishaan and Meher are best friends. Every day, they walk to school together, study in the same class, and play cricket after homework. One day, a teacher announces a leadership competition. Ishaan's name gets called out right away. Meher waits... but no one calls her name.

At lunch, Meher sighs, "I wanted to join too, but maybe leadership roles are more for boys." Ishaan looks confused. "Why would you think that?"

This moment shows what many children face daily—not from rules, but from beliefs that limit them. Welcome to the world where gender equality makes a difference.

Explore

What is Gender Equality?
Gender Equality means that all people—regardless of their gender—have the same rights, responsibilities, and opportunities.
This doesn't mean everyone is the same. It means everyone is treated with the same respect, offered the same chances, and protected by the same rules.

Gender equality is about fairness. It is when:
- Girls and boys are allowed to play any game they choose.
- Everyone gets equal chances to speak, learn, and lead.
- Boys can cook, cry, or paint—and no one laughs at them.
- Girls can climb trees, become scientists, or drive trucks—and everyone cheers them on!

Why Gender Equality Matters

Think about a garden where only one kind of flower gets sunlight and water. What happens to the rest?
That's what gender inequality does—it blocks the growth of people, especially girls, but sometimes boys too.
Benefits of Gender Equality:

Area	How It Helps
Education	More girls stay in school and learn confidently
Careers	Everyone can follow their passion and earn equally
Families	Chores and care work are shared fairly
Mental Health	Children feel accepted and supported
Society	Fairness leads to peace, growth, and unity

Inequality Today

Even today, gender inequality exists in many ways:
- Girls in some countries are forced to marry early.
- Boys are not allowed to show emotions.
- In movies, boys are the heroes; girls are side characters.
- Girls are told they can't be engineers.
- Boys are told they shouldn't like art or fashion.

These unfair differences are not always in rules—they are in people's minds. That's why we need to talk, learn, and change.

Understanding Equal vs. Identical

Equality does not mean that everyone must do the same things.
It means everyone should get equal respect and opportunity to choose what they want.

Not Equality	True Equality
All boys must do sports.	Boys and girls can choose sports or art.
Girls only help in the kitchen.	Everyone helps with home chores.
Boys always lead school assemblies.	Anyone can lead—based on skill and interest.

Try It

Activity 1: Spot the Fair and Unfair

Look at these situations. Discuss with your group or write down:
Is it fair or unfair?
1. Only boys get to join the science club.
2. A girl becomes class monitor because of her leadership.

3. Boys cannot choose dance as a hobby.
4. A boy wins a cooking contest and everyone claps.
5. Girls are asked to clean while boys play.

If something is unfair, how would you make it better?

Activity 2: Equality Poster Challenge

Make a colorful poster titled "What Equality Looks Like".

Include drawings or phrases that show boys and girls doing the same:

- Playing
- Studying
- Leading
- Expressing emotions
- Sharing responsibilities

Hang it in your classroom or home!

Activity 3: Equality at Home
Make a "Who Does What?" **table with chores like:**

- Setting the table
- Sweeping the floor
- Helping siblings
- Watering plants
- Repair work

Now ask: Who usually does each task in your family?
Next: Try switching one chore with a different family member and observe what happens!

Think & Reflect

1. Have you ever felt treated differently because of your gender?
2. Do you think girls and boys are treated equally in school? Why or

why not?
3. Why is it important for boys to also support gender equality?
4. Can gender equality help people be happier? How?

These questions build your social awareness—a key life skill!

Let's Revise

• Gender equality means everyone gets the same chances, choices, and respect, regardless of gender.
• It does not mean everyone is the same—it means everyone is valued equally.
• Inequality can exist in rules, roles, media, and mindsets.
• Equality benefits everyone—in school, home, health, work, and the world.
• Change starts with us.

Check Yourself

Choose the correct answer:

1. Gender equality means:

(a) Girls are better than boys
(b) Everyone gets equal chances ✔
(c) Only girls should study
(d) Only boys should work

2. Which of these shows gender equality?

(a) Only boys play cricket
(b) Girls are not allowed in the science lab
(c) Anyone can choose their favorite activity ✔
(d) Boys don't cry

3. True or False:

o Boys and girls must do the same things to be equal. ✗
o Gender equality helps everyone feel free and respected. ✔

Short Answer:

1. Name one area where you have seen gender inequality.
2. How can you support equality at school?
3. Why is it important to treat all genders with respect?

Beyond the Book

Mini Project: Equality Interview

Interview 3 classmates or neighbors using these questions:

- What does gender equality mean to you?
- Do you think boys and girls are treated the same in your community?
- What changes would you like to see?

Record their answers and write a paragraph about what you learned.

Digital Extension (QR Code Placeholder)

Watch: "Why Gender Equality Matters" – A short animation explaining equality using kids' voices from around the world.

Final Thought

Gender equality is not just about girls getting rights. It's about everyone—girls, boys, and all genders—living freely, equally, and respectfully.

When children grow up believing in fairness, they create a future that's more kind, more smart, and more powerful.

So the next time someone says, "That's not for girls" or "That's not for boys,"

you can smile and say,

"Actually, it's for everyone."

Chapter 3

Spot the Stereotype

Let's Begin

What Do You See First?

Look at these two images:

- In one picture, a girl is cooking, and a boy is playing football.
- In another, a boy is painting his nails, and a girl is fixing a bicycle.

Now answer:

Which one feels "normal"? Which one seems "funny" or "strange"? Why do you think that is?

We've grown up hearing and seeing certain things that tell us what boys and girls "should" do. But are these things always right? Or are they stereotypes?

Let's find out!

Explore

What is a Stereotype?
A stereotype is a belief or idea about a group of people that may not be true for everyone.

When it comes to gender, gender stereotypes are fixed ideas about how boys and girls are supposed to behave, dress, or think—just because of their gender.

For example:
- "Boys are better at math."
- "Girls like pink."
- "Boys don't cry."
- "Girls gossip more."

These are not facts. These are generalizations. And they can hurt.

Where Do Stereotypes Come From?

Stereotypes are all around us:

Source	Examples
Family	"Boys help outside; girls help in the kitchen."
Cartoons	Superheroes are boys; princesses are helpless girls.
Ads	Only moms doing laundry or cooking.
School	Teachers calling boys for lifting heavy things, girls for decorating.
Friends	"You play like a girl!" as an insult.

Over time, we start to believe these messages—even if they're false.

Why Stereotypes Are a Problem

They stop us from being our true selves.
They make us feel ashamed or weak.
They hurt confidence and create unfair rules.

Here's how stereotypes affect people:

Stereotype	Effect
Boys shouldn't cry	Boys hide feelings; feel lonely
Girls are bad at sports	Girls stop playing; miss out on fitness and fun
Only boys are tech-savvy	Girls avoid computers or science careers
Girls clean, boys relax	Unequal house responsibilities
Boys don't cook	Miss learning important life skills

Breaking the Box

The truth is:
✔ Boys can love poetry.
✔ Girls can be scientists.
✔ Anyone can wear pink, blue, yellow, or black.
✔ Emotions, interests, and dreams have no gender.

Gender stereotypes are like invisible boxes. But guess what? You have the power to break them.

Try It

Activity 1: "Is This a Stereotype?"
Below are some statements. Mark them as:

- ✔ Fair and Respectful
- ✗ A Stereotype

1. Boys are better at computers.
2. Girls like shopping more than boys.
3. Anyone can be a great leader.
4. Girls can't climb trees.
5. Boys shouldn't play with dolls.
6. Everyone can enjoy dancing.

Now review your answers with your class or family. Why are the stereotypes unfair?

Activity 2: Break the Box Poster
Make a two-part poster titled **"Stereotype vs Reality."**
- On the left, draw a common stereotype.
- On the right, draw a real-life example that breaks it.

Examples:
- **Left:** Girl = cleaning
- **Right:** Girl = fixing a car
- **Left:** Boy = strong hero
- **Right:** Boy = caring nurse

Display the poster in school for Gender Equality Week!

Activity 3: Rewrite the Story
Choose a well-known fairy tale or cartoon.

Now change one character's role to break a stereotype. For example:
- A prince trapped in a tower.
- A princess who rescues a knight.
- A superhero mom.

Write a paragraph about how this story sends a new message.

Think & Reflect

Ask yourself:

1. What is one stereotype I believed before but now question?
2. Have I ever judged someone based on their gender?
3. Have I been judged or teased for doing something “not typical”?
4. How can I support a friend who is different from what people expect?

Reflecting helps us grow kinder, more open, and more fair.

Let’s Revise

- A gender stereotype is a fixed, often unfair belief about boys, girls, or other genders.
- Stereotypes come from what we see in families, media, schools, and culture.
- These ideas can limit choices, lower self-confidence, and create unfairness.
- You can break stereotypes by questioning them and showing that anyone can do anything.
- It’s cool to be yourself—even if that means doing something others don’t expect!

Check Yourself

Multiple Choice:

1. What is a stereotype?

(a) A law
(b) A rule for school
(c) A fixed idea about people ✔
(d) A new toy

2. Which of the following is NOT a stereotype?
(a) Boys shouldn't wear pink
(b) Girls can be engineers ✔
(c) Boys are always noisy
(d) Girls love makeup

3. True or False:
- o Stereotypes can hurt people. ✔
- o Only girls suffer because of stereotypes. ✗
- o It's okay for boys to cry. ✔

Short Answer:
1. Write one gender stereotype you've heard.
2. Why do you think it is not true?
3. What can you do when you hear a friend say a stereotypical statement?

Beyond the Book

Mini Project: Stereotype Detective

This week, become a Stereotype Detective.
• Watch one TV show or advertisement.
• Write down: Who is doing what? Who is shown as strong, smart, caring, or silly?
• Does it show boys and girls equally?
• What message does it send?
At the end of the week, write one idea on how this story could be more fair and equal.

Digital Extension (QR Code Placeholder)

Watch: "Breaking the Gender Box" – A video where kids from around the world talk about gender stereotypes they've faced and how they challenged them.

Final Thought

A stereotype is like a fence built in our minds. It tells us, "Stay inside. Don't try that. **That's not for you."**

But you? You're not meant to be boxed in. You're meant to be free, bold, and limitless.

So, the next time someone says,
"That's not for boys" or "Girls don't do that,"
take a deep breath, smile, and say:
"Anyone can do anything. Watch me."

Chapter 4

Boys Can, Girls Can, Everyone Can!

Let's Begin

Two Dreams, Two Reactions
Zoya wants to become a firefighter. When she shares her dream at school, some kids laugh and say, "But girls can't do that—it's dangerous!"

Sameer wants to become a dance teacher. When he tells his cousins, they tease him, "That's a girl thing!"

Zoya and Sameer are just two kids with big dreams. But gender stereotypes are trying to stop them. The truth? Everyone should be free to dream, try, and succeed—no matter their gender.

This chapter is all about one powerful message:
If you can dream it, you can do it.

Explore

What Does "Everyone Can" Really Mean?

"Everyone Can" means that your choices, skills, dreams, or personality should not be judged based on your gender.

Some people think:
• Boys should only like action or adventure.
• Girls should always be quiet and neat.
• Boys should choose sports, and girls should pick arts.
• Boys are made to lead, and girls to follow.
These ideas are outdated and unfair.

The truth is:
• Girls can be brave, bold, loud, and strong.
• Boys can be gentle, emotional, creative, and kind.
• People of all genders can do any job, play any role, and shine in any field.

Real-Life Examples of Breaking the Mold

Let's look at some inspiring people who didn't let gender stop them.

Name	What They Did	Why It Matters
Kalpana Chawla	First Indian woman in space	Proved space isn't just for men
Mary Kom	World boxing champion	Fought and won in a male-dominated sport
Gaurav Tomar	Male ballet dancer	Chose grace over stereotypes
Dr. Tessy Thomas	Missile scientist	Known as India's "Missile Woman"

Arunima Sinha	First female amputee to climb Mt. Everest	Redefined courage and strength
Kiran Bedi	First female IPS officer	Broke barriers in law enforcement

These people didn't ask, **"Is this for my gender?"**
They asked, "Is this my passion?"—and they followed it.

Understanding Gender and Ability

There is no such thing as a "boy skill" or "girl skill."
• Courage has no gender.
• Leadership has no gender.
• Creativity has no gender.
• Intelligence has no gender.
• Kindness has no gender.

What matters most is:
• Interest: What do I love doing?
• Effort: Am I ready to learn and try?
• Support: Do I help others grow too?

Equal Doesn't Mean Same

Boys and girls are not identical—they may have different interests or experiences—but that doesn't mean one is better, weaker, or limited.

Equality means:
• All children are free to express themselves.
• All children are given the chance to try.
• All children are praised for who they are—not what society expects them to be.

Try It

Activity 1: “Mix the Match”

Look at the following careers. Write who can do each: Boys, Girls, or Everyone?

Job	Who Can Do It?
Pilot	?
Teacher	?
Farmer	?
Nurse	?
Astronaut	?
Chef	?
Dancer	?
Builder	?

Answer: Everyone!
Let’s remove labels from jobs.

Activity 2: Create a “Dream Wall”

On a large sheet or classroom wall:
1. Write down your dream job or future goal.
2. Decorate it with drawings, stickers, or cut-outs.

3. Add the sentence:
“I can do it because my dreams don’t have a gender.”
Encourage everyone to read each other’s dreams and celebrate them.

Activity 3: “Switch the Story”
Choose a scene from a book or cartoon where boys are heroes or girls are quiet side characters.

Now rewrite it:

• Make the girl the leader or rescuer.
• Make the boy the caregiver or artist.
• Change who solves the problem—and how.

You can even act it out!

Think & Reflect

Ask yourself:

1. Have I ever hidden my interest because someone said "That's not for boys/girls"?
2. Do I encourage friends when they choose something different?
3. What would the world be like if we all supported each other's dreams?
4. Can I be a role model who breaks gender norms?

Write a short reflection: "What would I do if there were no gender rules?"

Let's Revise

• Every person, no matter their gender, should have the freedom to choose their path.
• Stereotypes try to say "only boys can do this" or "only girls can do that"—but they're wrong.
• Real people break barriers every day. So can you.
• What matters most is your effort, interest, and heart—not your gender.
• Supporting others in their choices is also part of gender equality.

Check Yourself

Multiple Choice Questions:

1. Who can be a scientist?
(a) Only boys

(b) Only girls
(c) Anyone who loves science ✔
(d) Only men with glasses

2. Which statement is correct?
(a) Boys can't be nurses
(b) Girls are not strong enough for sports
(c) Anyone can lead a team ✔
(d) Girls can't climb trees

3. True or False:
- o A boy can love dancing. ✔
- o Only girls can care for babies. ✗
- o Everyone should follow their dreams. ✔

Beyond the Book

Project: "Inspiring People Around Me"

Find one person in your neighborhood, family, or community who does something unusual for their gender.

For example:
- • A woman mechanic
- • A male nurse
- • A girl who plays football on a boys' team
- • A father who stays home to care for kids

Ask them:
1. What do they do?
2. Why did they choose it?
3. Did anyone discourage them?
4. What kept them going?

Write a short report or create a presentation about them.

Digital Extension (QR Code Placeholder)

Watch: "Girls Can, Boys Can, Everyone Can" – A video of children breaking stereotypes and sharing their talents proudly.

Final Thought

The world is full of colors, talents, dreams, and ideas. Why limit them with gender rules?
Zoya can be a firefighter. Sameer can be a dance teacher. You can be anything you want to be.
So let's say it together:

"Boys can. Girls can. Everyone can!"

Chapter 5

Home, School, Playground

Equality Everywhere

Let's Begin

Same Class, Different Treatment
Arya and Rohan are classmates. They both love math, enjoy football, and help their families at home. But Arya always gets asked to arrange the classroom flowers. Rohan is asked to carry heavy books. During lunch, Arya's mom tells her to help wash the dishes while Rohan's brother plays video games.

Arya wonders, "Why do I always have to do these things just because I'm a girl?"

Rohan wonders, "Why don't they let me decorate or help in the kitchen?"
If you've ever felt something similar, this chapter is for you.

Explore

At Home: Small Habits, Big Impact
Home is where we learn our first lessons—how to speak, care, share, and respect.
But sometimes, unequal habits begin here too.

Think about it:
• Are girls asked to cook more than boys?
• Are boys told not to cry, even when they are upset?
• Are chores divided based on gender?
When responsibilities and expectations are based only on gender, it becomes unfair.

Ask:
"Is this task for everyone, or just for one gender?"
"Why can't we all learn every skill—cooking, cleaning, fixing, or helping?"

Equality at Home looks like:
• Everyone sharing chores fairly.
• Parents treating all children with equal encouragement.
• Brothers and sisters learning from each other.
• Boys learning care, and girls learning confidence.

At School: Learning Respect and Fairness

School is not just about books—it's where we learn values and life skills. But sometimes, **even schools follow old patterns:**

Situation	What Often Happens	What Should Happen
Group leader selection	Boys are chosen to lead	Everyone should get a chance

Dance or drama	Girls are picked	All students should be invited
Science and tech clubs	More boys join	Encourage all genders equally
Cleaning or decoration	Girls are asked more	Chores should be shared

Teachers, classmates, and school leaders can make a big difference by showing that respect and responsibility belong to everyone.

On the Playground: Where Equality Should Run Free

Play is fun—but also powerful. It teaches teamwork, fairness, and freedom.

But have you heard:
- "Girls don't play cricket."
- "Boys shouldn't jump rope."
- "Girls are not strong enough to climb."

These ideas are limiting. The playground should be a place where everyone:
- Chooses their game.
- Gets equal turns.
- Competes with fun, not bias.
- Learns how to win and lose with respect.

Encourage mix-gender teams. Praise effort, not gender. Play to include, not exclude.

Why Everyday Equality Matters

Equality isn't just about big rules or laws.

It's about small actions—who you listen to, share with, support, and trust.

Wherever we go—home, school, or outside—equality means:
• Everyone's time and ideas matter.
• Everyone gets a chance to speak and lead.
• Everyone can choose how to express themselves.
When you create equality in your space, you become a real-life changemaker.

Try It

Activity 1: Equality Checklist
Look around your home or classroom. Tick ✔ the ones that happen:
• Boys and girls share chores
• Everyone is allowed to speak in class
• Girls and boys play together
• All students are encouraged to lead
• All voices are heard and respected

Now ask:
• What can we do about the ✗ boxes?
• How can we turn those into next week?

Activity 2: Role-Reversal Day
Choose one day to swap tasks or roles:
• Boys do what girls usually do
• Girls take on typical "boy roles"
• Everyone reflects on the experience

At the end of the day, write:
• "What surprised me?"
• "What did I learn about fairness?"

Activity 3: Chore Board

Create a Chore Sharing Board for home or classroom:

- List 10 common tasks
- Assign them randomly or rotate them weekly
- Include everyone—no task is "for boys only" or "for girls only"

This builds teamwork and equality in everyday life.

Think & Reflect

Take time to think:

1. Who does most of the work at home?
2. Are boys and girls treated the same in your school?
3. Have you ever felt left out because of your gender?
4. What is one small thing you can do to make your space fairer?

Write a reflection titled:

"What I Want My Home and School to Look Like"

Let's Revise

- Gender equality should exist not just in rules, but in daily life—at home, in school, and on playgrounds.
- Everyone can help in all ways—chores, leadership, games, and group work.
- Unfair treatment starts with small habits, but so does fairness.
- We must question habits that are based on "he does this, she does that."
- Respect, sharing, and encouragement are for all.

Check Yourself

Multiple Choice:

1. Which of the following is a sign of equality?

(a) Only boys clean blackboards

(b) Girls always decorate the classroom

(c) Everyone gets a chance to lead ✔
(d) Boys play outside, girls stay in

2. What should be shared at home?
(a) Only food
(b) Responsibilities ✔
(c) Toys only among boys
(d) None of the above

3. True or False:
- o Girls should not play football ✗
- o Boys can help in the kitchen ✔
- o Chores can be shared fairly ✔

Short Answer:
1. What is one thing you do at home that supports gender equality?
2. What's one school rule you'd like to change to make it more equal?
3. How would you include everyone during a game?

Beyond the Book

Project: Equality Champions Journal

Keep a 1-week journal with these questions:
- Did I treat everyone fairly today?
- Did I speak up when I saw something unfair?
- Did I share work, space, or ideas with someone of a different gender?
- Did I stop myself from judging someone based on gender?

Write 3 sentences each day. Share what you learned at the end of the week.

Digital Extension (QR Code Placeholder)

Watch: "Equality Starts at Home" – A short video showing children around the world sharing chores, learning, and leadership—together.

Final Thought

You don't need to change the whole world to fight inequality.
You can start at your dining table, classroom desk, or playground corner.
When you treat others with fairness, respect, and kindness, you build a better world for everyone.
So let's promise today:

"In my home, my school, and my games—everyone is equal."

Chapter 6

Words Matter – Language and Respect

Let's Begin

"Don't be such a girl!"
"Man up!"
"You throw like a girl!"

Have you heard these phrases before? Maybe you've even used them without thinking.

Now ask yourself—how do they make someone feel?
Sometimes, the words we use seem small, but they leave a big impact. This chapter is about understanding how language shapes equality—and how you can use words to spread respect instead of stereotypes.

Explore

Why Words Matter

Words can do two things:
• Build people up – make them feel strong, valued, and confident
• Tear people down – make them feel weak, different, or ashamed

Language teaches people how to think and behave. If we hear certain messages again and again, we start to believe them—even if they're untrue or unfair.

For example:
• Saying "girls are bossy" can make girls feel bad for being leaders.
• Saying "real boys don't cry" can make boys hide their feelings.
• Calling someone "too girly" or "not manly enough" can cause shame or bullying.

Language teaches what is 'normal'—so it's important that our words show respect, fairness, and inclusion.

Harmful Phrases to Avoid

Here are some common phrases that sound harmless but actually support gender stereotypes:

Harmful Phrase	What's the Problem?
"Be a man!"	Suggests boys can't be soft, emotional, or scared
"You're acting like a girl."	Treats girl behavior as weak or silly
"She's so bossy."	Punishes girls for leadership
"Girls are too sensitive."	Makes emotions seem wrong

“That’s women’s work.”	Belittles domestic work and limits who can do what
“Boys will be boys.”	Excuses bad behavior instead of correcting it

These words may seem small, but they grow into big walls of inequality.

Respectful Language to Use

Here are better ways to say things that show support and fairness:

Instead of...	Say...
“Man up!”	“You can handle this. I believe in you.”
“You throw like a girl.”	“Great try! Let’s keep practicing.”
“She’s bossy.”	“She’s confident and speaks her mind.”
“That’s not for boys.”	“Everyone should try what they enjoy.”
“Stop crying like a girl.”	“It’s okay to cry. Want to talk?”
“Thanks to the ladies for cleaning.”	“Thanks to everyone who helped.”

Using inclusive language helps everyone feel respected, equal, and seen.

Gender-Neutral Terms

We often use job titles or roles that suggest a certain gender. Let's fix that!

Old Term	Inclusive Term
Policeman	Police officer
Fireman	Firefighter
Chairman	Chairperson
Stewardess	Flight attendant
Businessman	Businessperson
Mankind	Humankind or Humanity

Words shape what we see as possible. Let's make sure every child sees themselves in every role.

Try It

Activity 1: Word Swap Game

Take each sentence and make it inclusive:
1. "Girls aren't strong." → ____________________
2. "Only boys play video games." → ____________________
3. "He cries too much. What a girl!" → _______________
4. "Dad is the boss of the house." → ____________________
5. "All policemen were brave." → ____________________

Now think: How did the new sentence feel different?

Activity 2: Create a "Words That Respect" Poster

Step 1: Fold a large sheet into two sides.
• On one side, write "Hurtful Phrases" and add examples (with

crossed-out signs).
• On the other, write "Respectful Language" and show better versions with smiley faces or colorful icons.

Step 2: Decorate it and display it in your classroom, home, or community area.

Goal: Make people think before they speak.

Activity 3: Dialogue Rewrite
Choose a short conversation from a cartoon or book where a character uses a gender-biased phrase.
Rewrite the dialogue using respectful language.

Perform both versions with your friends or classmates and ask:
• Which version made people feel included?
• Which one felt hurtful or awkward?

Think & Reflect

Ask yourself:
1. Have I ever used a gendered phrase without realizing it?
2. How would I feel if someone used those words about me?
3. How can I speak in a way that makes everyone feel equal?

Write a short paragraph:
"Three words I will stop using, and three I will start using."

Let's Revise

• Language has power—it teaches, includes, or excludes.
• Stereotypes grow when we repeat hurtful or limiting phrases.
• Using inclusive words makes everyone feel safe and valued.
• We can replace gendered job titles and harmful phrases with respectful alternatives.

• Being mindful of words is a daily practice and part of building a fair world.

Check Yourself

Multiple Choice:

1. What is a stereotype-supporting phrase?
(a) "You are brave."
(b) "She's too bossy." ✔
(c) "Everyone is allowed to try."
(d) "Would you like help with that?"

2. Which is a gender-neutral job title?
(a) Businessman
(b) Policeman
(c) Chairperson ✔
(d) Fireman

3. True or False:
- o Words can make someone feel excluded. ✔
- o "Boys don't cry" is a helpful phrase. ✗
- o Language can promote fairness. ✔

Short Answer:
1. Write two phrases you hear often that are unfair.
2. How would you rewrite them respectfully?
3. Why should we avoid gender-based jokes or insults?

Beyond the Book

Project: "Word Watch Journal"

For one week, keep a journal. Write down:
• Any gendered or stereotype-based words you hear.

• Who said them (no names, just who—teacher, TV, friend, etc.).
• How it made someone feel.
• What could have been said instead?
At the end of the week, present your learnings to your class or family.

Be the "Language Leader" in your group!

Digital Extension (QR Code Placeholder)

Watch: "Words Can Build or Break" – A video where children around the world share the phrases that made them feel small—and how kind words changed everything.

Final Thought

Words are like seeds. When you speak with care and kindness, you grow a garden of respect around you.

So the next time you speak, ask:
"Are my words helping someone grow?"
"Am I lifting others or pushing them down?"

Use your voice to say:
"I choose words that respect, include, and uplift."

Chapter 7

Real Stories of Role Models

Let's Begin

Imagine a girl who wanted to go to school but was told, "Girls don't need education."
Now imagine that same girl growing up to change the world.
Imagine a boy who loved dancing but was teased for being "too girly."
Now imagine him dancing on the biggest stage, inspiring millions.
Real heroes are not just in comic books. They are people—like you—who stood up against unfair rules and gender stereotypes.
Let's meet some real-life role models who prove that equality is possible and powerful.

Explore

Why Role Models Matter
Role models are people we admire and learn from.
They inspire us to believe that we can do anything—no matter our gender.

But for many years, people were told:
• "This job is for men."
• "Girls shouldn't be leaders."
• "Boys can't do that."

These ideas stop dreams.
Role models break these barriers.

They say: "Yes, we can!"
Let's meet some of them.

Malala Yousafzai – The Voice for Girls' Education

Country: Pakistan
Nobel Peace Prize Winner (youngest ever)
Malala loved going to school. But in her town, some people wanted to stop girls from studying. They closed schools and told girls to stay home.

Malala spoke up. Even though it was dangerous, she said:
"Every girl has a right to learn."
She was attacked, but she survived—and kept fighting.
Today, Malala travels the world, helping millions of girls go to school.

Her words:
"One child, one teacher, one book, one pen can change the world."

Serena Williams – Breaking Records and Bias

Country: USA
23 Grand Slam Tennis Titles
Serena faced racism and gender bias. People said she was too strong, too loud, too different. But Serena didn't stop. She became one of the greatest athletes in the world.

She showed that girls can be powerful, bold, and successful in sports.

Lesson: "You don't have to fit into someone's box. Break it and shine."

Marie Curie – Science Has No Gender

Country: Poland/France
First woman to win a Nobel Prize (and only person to win in two sciences!)
In the 1900s, women were not welcome in science labs. Marie Curie changed that.
She studied radioactive elements and helped in the discovery of new medicines and X-rays. She proved that intelligence has no gender.
Her story teaches us: "Curiosity and hard work can break any barrier."

Billy Porter – Redefining Fashion and Masculinity

Country: USA
Actor, singer, fashion icon
Billy wears tuxedos with gowns. He paints his nails. He sings, dances, and speaks out for equal rights.
People mocked him for not dressing "like a man." But Billy replied, "This is me—and that's enough."
He teaches us that you can be strong, soft, stylish, or serious—no matter your gender.

Kalpana Saroj – From Poverty to Business Icon

Country: India
Padma Shri Awardee
As a Dalit girl, Kalpana faced many challenges—poverty, discrimination, and a child marriage. But she fought back. She worked hard, started her own business, and became the head of

Kamani Tubes, a big company.
She is known as India's original "Slumdog Millionaire."
Kalpana proved that no background can stop a brave mind.

Ravi – The Boy Who Loved Dolls

Fictional story based on many real boys
Ravi loved dolls, art, and storytelling. But kids in his class laughed at him. They said, "Dolls are for girls."
Ravi felt sad. But one day, his art teacher saw his drawings and said, "You have a gift!"

Years later, Ravi became a famous designer, creating dolls that looked like kids from all around the world.
Ravi teaches us: "There's no such thing as a boy's toy or a girl's dream."

Try It

Activity 1: My Role Model Collage
Step 1: Choose 3 role models (famous or from your life).

Step 2: Write their names, what they did, and how they broke gender norms.

Step 3: Paste their pictures or draw them in your notebook.

Step 4: Share with your class!

Ask: "What can I learn from them?"

Activity 2: "I Am a Role Model" Poster
Draw yourself doing something that breaks a stereotype.

Examples:

• A girl playing cricket.
• A boy baking a cake.
•A child becoming a coder, leader, or pilot.

Write:

"I am strong, kind, and fearless. I am a role model."
Display your poster at home or in class.

Activity 3: Interview a Role Model
Find someone around you—a parent, teacher, neighbor—who challenges gender roles.

Ask:

• What challenges did they face?
• How did they overcome them?
• What advice do they have for kids today?

Write a short report and present it as a mini-biography.

Think & Reflect

Ask yourself:

1. Who inspires me the most? Why?
2. Have I ever stopped myself from doing something because of my gender?
3. What would I do if I were not afraid of being judged?

Write a paragraph:
"If I were truly free, I would..."

Let's Revise

• Role models teach us to dream big, no matter our gender.
• From science to sports, business to fashion—everyone belongs everywhere.

• Real heroes stand up against unfairness and help others rise.
• You don't have to be famous to be a role model—you can start today.

Check Yourself

Multiple Choice:

1. Who is the youngest Nobel Peace Prize winner?
(a) Marie Curie
(b) Malala Yousafzai ✔
(c) Kalpana Saroj
(d) Serena Williams

2. Which role model is known for science?
(a) Serena Williams
(b) Billy Porter
(c) Marie Curie ✔
(d) Ravi

3. True or False:
- o Girls can't play cricket ✗
- o Boys can love art and dolls ✔
- o One person can inspire many ✔

Short Answer:
1. Name one female and one male role model you admire.
2. What stereotype did they break?
3. How did they inspire you?

Beyond the Book

Project:
Create a Gender Equality Hall of Fame
1. Make a wall or digital slideshow.
2. Add pictures and facts about inspiring people who broke gender

stereotypes.
3. Include famous people and local heroes.

Invite classmates or family to contribute!

Digital Extension (QR Code Placeholder)

Watch: "Be Your Own Hero" – A short documentary of young children across India choosing non-traditional dreams—from girl bike mechanics to boy nurses.

Final Thought

You don't need superpowers to be a hero. You just need courage to be yourself—**and kindness to lift others.**

So ask yourself today:
"What dream do I have?"
"Will I let a stereotype stop me?"
Say it loud:

"I can be anything I want to be—because I am equal."

Chapter 8

Equality Beyond Gender

Respecting All Differences

Let's Begin

Think about your classroom.
Are all your friends the same height, same skin tone, same voice, or even from the same religion?

Of course not!
Now imagine a world where everyone looked and thought exactly alike.

Wouldn't that be boring?
This chapter is about understanding that equality is not just about gender—it's about respecting every kind of difference: skin color, religion, language, ability, background, and more.

We are all equal in value, even if we are different in many ways.

Explore

What Is Diversity?
Diversity means difference. It could be:
• Where someone comes from
• What language they speak
• What food they eat
• Their religion or beliefs
• Their family background
• Their abilities and challenges

The world is a rainbow of people. And every color matters.
When we respect diversity, we make our communities fair, kind, and strong.

Why Equality Is Bigger Than Gender

You've already learned how girls and boys should be treated equally.
But equality also means:
• A child with a disability should get the same chance to play and learn.
• A boy from a tribal area should have the same right to a good school.
• A girl who doesn't speak English well should not be laughed at.
• A child with dark skin should not be teased or excluded.

Equality is not everyone being the same, but everyone being treated with the same respect.

Understanding Bias and Prejudice

Let's learn two important words:

Term	What It Means
Bias	A quick judgment about someone without knowing them fully
Prejudice	An unfair opinion formed about a person or group

For example:

• Thinking girls aren't good at math is a gender bias.
• Believing someone from a village can't speak well is a class prejudice.
• Laughing at someone's accent is a language bias.

When we spot our own biases and unlearn them, we grow kinder.

Equality vs. Equity

Another important idea is the difference between equality and equity.

Equality	Equity
Giving everyone the same	Giving everyone what they need to succeed

Imagine:

• Three children of different heights trying to look over a wall.
• If all get the same stool (equality), the shortest still can't see.
• But if each gets the stool size they need (equity), everyone sees over the wall.

We must support others based on what they need, not just treat everyone identically.

Try It

Activity 1: Equality for All

Create a table with three columns:

Name	What Makes Them Different	What They Deserve
A friend who stammers	Speaks slowly	Patience and respect

A girl who wears a headscarf	Religion and dress	Safety and dignity
A boy who uses a wheelchair	Physical ability	Equal play and access

Add more rows based on people you know.

Think: "How can I support them?"

Activity 2: Roleplay – "What Would You Do?"

Split into groups and act out scenarios like:

1. A new student is shy and speaks a different language.
2. A boy wants to join the dance team, but others tease him.
3. A girl with dark skin is being called names.
4. A child with hearing loss is being left out of a game.

After each skit, discuss:

- What was unfair?
- How did it make them feel?
- What could you say or do instead?

Activity 3: Design a "Respect Badge"
Design a badge that shows you stand for equality and respect for all.

Add symbols for different:

- Genders
- Religions
- Abilities
- Languages
- Cultures

Write a pledge: "I respect all differences and stand up for fairness."

Think & Reflect

Ask yourself:
1. Have I ever judged someone because they were different?
2. What makes me unique—and how do I want to be treated?
3. What will I do if I see someone being bullied or teased?

Write a reflection:
"Three ways I will show respect to others who are different from me."

Let's Revise

- Equality includes gender, but also race, religion, language, ability, and more.
- Everyone deserves respect, safety, and opportunity—regardless of differences.
- Bias and prejudice harm individuals and communities.
- Equity helps everyone succeed by meeting their needs.
- You can be an equality champion by listening, learning, and standing up for others.

Check Yourself

Multiple Choice:
1. What does "diversity" mean?
(a) Everyone is the same
(b) Everyone is different and that's okay ✔
(c) Only boys and girls are equal
(d) One religion is better than others

2. What is "bias"?
(a) Treating all people with love
(b) A fair decision
(c) A quick, unfair judgment ✔
(d) A type of hairstyle

3. True or False:

o All people should be treated with respect ✔

o Dark skin is less beautiful ✗

o Different needs require different supports ✔

Short Answer:

1. Name one way people are different.
2. How can we treat them fairly?
3. Why is it important to accept differences?

Beyond the Book

Project: "Equality Tree"

Step 1: Draw or create a large tree with many branches.

Step 2: On each leaf, write or draw one way people are different.

Step 3: Under each leaf, write a way to show respect.

Your tree becomes a symbol of inclusion in your classroom or home.

Digital Extension (QR Code Placeholder)

Watch: "We're Different, We're the Same" – A children's video that shows how our hearts and feelings are the same, even when we look different on the outside.

Final Thought

You may not always understand someone's life, but you can always choose kindness.

Next time you see someone who is different, say to yourself:

"I don't have to be the same as you to respect you."

"Our differences make the world colorful."

Say it proudly:

"I stand for all. I respect all. We rise together."

Chapter 9

From Home to School

Creating Equal Spaces Everywhere

Let's Begin

Think about your day:
You wake up at home.
You get ready and go to school.
You meet friends, learn, play, and return home.

But have you ever noticed if boys and girls are treated the same in these places?
Who does the cooking? Who carries heavy things?
Who is asked to be quiet? Who leads the classroom group?
Equality doesn't just happen in speeches or books.
It must live in homes, schools, playgrounds, and everywhere else we go.
Let's learn how we can create equal spaces where everyone feels safe, respected, and valued.

Explore

Equality at Home
Home is where we first learn about the world.
It's where we pick up habits, values, and ideas.

But sometimes, even without meaning to, families treat boys and girls differently:
• Girls are asked to clean, cook, or serve tea.
• Boys are allowed to play or rest while chores are done.
• Girls are told to speak softly; boys are told to "be tough."
These are gender roles, and they limit both boys and girls.

What Can We Do?
• Share chores equally—boys can cook, girls can fix things.
• Talk openly about fairness.
• **Ask:** "Would I ask this if it were a boy?" or "Would I expect this if it were a girl?"
Even small actions—like letting a girl choose what to wear or asking a boy how he feels—can create a fair and loving home.

Equality at School

School is not just a place to study.
It's where children learn to lead, speak, share, question, and grow.

But even in school, we may see unfair treatment:
• Boys may be chosen more often to lead teams or sports.
• Girls may be told they're not good at math or science.
• Boys may be laughed at for dancing or showing emotions.
• Children who are different may be teased or ignored.

Equality means:
• Everyone gets a chance to speak.
• All subjects and sports are for all.

• Differences are respected, not mocked.
Teachers, too, play a big role. They must treat all students with fairness and encourage everyone equally.

Home and School: Working Together

A child who feels equal at home will act fairly at school.
A school that teaches equality will inspire change at home.

Both places must:

- Listen to children's voices
- Encourage equal participation
- Correct stereotypes and unfair habits

For example:

- If a girl loves science, her family and teachers must support her.
- If a boy wants to act in a play, he should be praised, not teased.

Equal spaces raise confident, caring, and brave children.

Try It

Activity 1: Family Equality Checklist
With your parents or guardians, tick off what applies in your home:

Statement	No /Yes
Boys and girls do house chores equally	✗ / ✔
Everyone is encouraged to speak up	✗ / ✔
Toys are shared freely	✗ / ✔
No one is made fun of for being different	✗ / ✔
Everyone is treated with kindness and respect	✗ / ✔

Now discuss: What can we do better?

Activity 2: Classroom Equality Circle

In your class:

1. Sit in a circle.
2. Each student answers:

"I feel equal at school when..."

"I feel unfairness when..."

Teachers can note down common points and create a classroom

Equality Code, like:

- We let everyone speak.
- We take turns leading.
- We stop jokes that hurt others.
- We stand up for each other.

Put the Equality Code on the classroom wall!

Activity 3: Equal Chores Game

Divide students into groups and give them chore cards like:

- Sweep the floor
- Water plants
- Sharpen pencils
- Carry sports equipment
- Hand out notebooks

Mix roles. Let girls carry, boys distribute, all students clean.

Then ask:

"Did anything surprise you?"

"How did it feel to do something new?"

Learning comes from doing.

Think & Reflect

Ask yourself:

1. Do I see fairness in how chores and tasks are shared at home?
2. Has someone ever stopped me from doing something because I'm a boy/girl?

3. What would an "equal classroom" look like?

Write your thoughts:
"Three things I will do to make home/school more equal."

Let's Revise

• Home and school are where children first learn equality.
• Gender roles at home can lead to inequality—sharing chores and decisions helps!
• Schools must give equal chances to speak, lead, learn, and play.
• Teachers and families must work together to build fairness.
• Equality is not just a rule—it's a habit we practice every day.

Check Yourself

Multiple Choice:

1. What is a sign of equality at home?
(a) Only girls cooking
(b) Boys fixing things alone
(c) Everyone sharing chores ✔
(d) Girls serving boys

2. What is a gender role?
(a) A type of movie
(b) An unfair idea about what boys/girls should do ✔
(c) A subject in school
(d) A homework sheet

3. True or False:
- o Equality must be taught in both home and school ✔
- o Only boys should be team leaders ✗
- o Girls can be good at science and sports ✔

Short Answer:

1. Name one thing that is unequal at home or school.
2. What can you do to change it?
3. Why is it important to be fair?

Beyond the Book

Project: Build a "Fairness Wall"

In class or at home:

- Take a large chart paper.
- Everyone adds sticky notes saying:
  - o One unfair thing they saw
  - o One fair thing they did

Every week, read the wall and celebrate improvements!

Digital Extension (QR Code Placeholder)

Watch: "The Equal Home" – A fun animated video that shows how a family learns to share chores and respect everyone's choices.

Final Thought

Every place can be a place of equality—if we make it so.
You don't need a rulebook or a loud voice. You just need to look

around and say:
"This isn't fair."
"Let's fix it together."
Say it proudly:
"My home, my school, my world—equal for all!"

Chapter 10

Be the Change

How Kids Can Be Equality Champions

Let's Begin

Have you ever stood up for someone being treated unfairly?
Have you ever shared something with a friend who felt left out?
Have you ever said, "That's not fair" when someone teased another kid?
If yes, then you've already taken the first step toward becoming a champion of equality.
This chapter is all about you.
Because real change begins not with governments or big speeches, but with small actions taken by young heroes like you.

Explore

Who Is an Equality Champion?
An Equality Champion is someone who:
- Treats all people with fairness and respect

- Speaks up when something is wrong
- Believes everyone deserves equal chances
- Encourages others to do the same

You don't need to be a teacher or a grown-up.
Children can lead big changes too.

The Qualities of a Champion

Let's look at the superpowers that make someone an Equality Champion:

Superpower	What It Looks Like
Kindness	Helping others feel welcome
Courage	Speaking up when something is wrong
Fairness	Including everyone in games and decisions
Listening	Understanding different points of view
Action	Turning ideas into real changes

These superpowers are not found in comic books.
They live in you.

Small Actions, Big Impact

Here are some real examples of how children like you make a difference:

- A girl asks the teacher why only boys were chosen for a science project.
- A boy invites a shy classmate to join his football team.
- A child writes a poem about how girls and boys are equally strong.
- A student makes a class poster with the words: "Respect All Differences."

Each act is a step toward a more equal world.

Know Your Rights, Respect Others' Rights

As a child, you have rights too!

According to UNICEF, every child has the right to:

• Education
• Health and safety
• Protection from discrimination
• Expression and participation

But with rights come responsibilities.

You must:

• Respect others' rights
• Speak kindly and fairly
• Stand against injustice

A true champion doesn't just know—they act.

Try It

Activity 1: My Equality Footprint
Draw two large footprints on paper.
In one, write what you already do to support equality.
In the other, write what you want to start doing.

Example:

• **Left Foot:** "I don't laugh at different clothes."
• **Right Foot:** "I want to speak up when someone is teased."

Paste it on your wall as your "Equality Steps."

Activity 2: Build an Equality Toolkit

Create a small booklet or poster with tools to use when you see inequality:

Situation	My Equality Tool
A classmate is teased for being different	“Stop, that’s not okay.”
Someone is left out of a group	“Let’s include them.”
A girl is told she can’t play cricket	“Everyone can play anything!”
A boy is crying and others say ‘Don’t be weak’	“Feelings are for everyone.”

Carry your toolkit in your mind every day!

Activity 3: I Am an Equality Champion – Roleplay

Create a short 1-minute speech starting with:
“I stand for equality because…”
Use your voice to inspire others!
Record it or present it to your class.

Encourage your school to organize a “Champion’s Day” where everyone shares ideas and actions for equality.

Think & Reflect

Ask yourself:

1. What is one unfair thing I’ve seen?
2. What did I do—or what could I have done?
3. How will I act differently next time?

Write your Equality Pledge:
“I promise to treat everyone fairly, speak up when something is wrong, and be kind always.”
Stick it where you can see it every morning!

Let's Revise

• Equality Champions are kids who believe in and act for fairness.
• You don't need to be big to make a big difference.
• Knowing your rights and standing up for others is powerful.
• Small actions—inviting, speaking kindly, sharing—can spark big changes.
• Your tools are kindness, courage, fairness, and respect.

Check Yourself

Multiple Choice:

1. What is NOT a quality of an equality champion?
(a) Kindness
(b) Bullying ✔
(c) Fairness
(d) Courage

2. What does UNICEF say every child has?
(a) Toys
(b) A pet
(c) Rights ✔
(d) A bicycle

3. True or False:
o Only teachers can stop bullying ✔
o Children can create equal spaces ✔
o Respect should only be given to friends ✔

Short Answer:
1. Write one action you will take to support gender equality.
2. What would you say if someone is being unfair?
3. Why is being an equality champion important?

Beyond the Book

Project: Equality Journal
Start a weekly journal titled:
"My Journey as an Equality Champion"

Each week, write:

- One thing I did for fairness
- One thing I saw that wasn't fair
- One way I can do better next time

After a month, share your journal with friends or family.
You'll see how your small steps lead to big change.

Digital Extension (QR Code Placeholder)

Watch: "Kids Can Make a Difference" – Stories of real children changing their communities.
Play: An interactive quiz called "Equality Hero" – Choose what you would do in different real-life situations.

Final Thought

You are brave. You are smart. You are strong.
And you have the power to make the world a better place.
You don't have to wait to grow up.
You can be the change—today.
So go ahead. Be the one who smiles first.
Be the one who invites everyone to play.
Be the one who says: "Let's make it fair."

Say it proudly:
"I am an Equality Champion—and I make the world equal for all."

Book Summary

All Are Equal

The Essential Gender Equality Guide

"All Are Equal" is a joyful and thoughtful journey into the world of gender equality — written especially for children in Grades 3–8. Through real-life examples, interactive activities, and inspiring stories, this book helps young readers understand what fairness means and how they can make a difference.

Each chapter explores key ideas:

• What gender is and why it matters
• What equality looks like in daily life
• How to spot and challenge stereotypes
• Why respect and kindness are important
• How homes, schools, and society can become fairer for all

With a focus on critical thinking, creative activities, and values-based learning, children learn how to respect differences, challenge unfairness, and become champions of change.

This book encourages:

• Open discussions with peers and adults
• Positive behavior toward all genders
• Leadership through fairness, empathy, and courage

It's more than a book—it's a toolkit for raising kind, fair, and inclusive citizens of tomorrow.

Glossary: Important Words to Remember

Word	Simple Meaning
Gender	How people see themselves and others as boys, girls, or other identities.
Sex	A person's biological body differences at birth (male or female).
Equality	Treating everyone the same and giving everyone equal chances.
Gender Equality	Boys, girls, and all genders have equal rights, opportunities, and respect.
Stereotype	A fixed idea that all people in a group are the same, like "boys are strong" or "girls are quiet."
Discrimination	Treating someone unfairly because of who they are, like their gender, race, or background.
Bias	Having a strong opinion or preference that may be unfair.
Feminism	The belief that men and women should have equal rights and opportunities.
Champion	Someone who supports and fights for a cause, like fairness or equality.
Inclusion	Making sure everyone feels welcome and part of the group.

Empathy	Understanding and caring about how someone else feels.
Role Model	A person whose behavior sets a good example for others.
Right	Something every person is allowed to have or do (like the right to education or safety).
Responsibility	A duty to do what is right or helpful.
Respect	Treating others kindly and thinking about their feelings.
Fairness	Making sure everyone is treated equally and justly.